For Amy!

Pumpkin Trouble

For information address HarperCollins Children's Books, a division of HarperCollins Publishers, 195 Broadway, New York, NY 10007.
www.harpercollinschildrens.com

Library of Congress Cataloging-in-Publication Data
Thomas, Jan, date
Pumpkin trouble / Jan Thomas. — 1st ed.
p. cm.
Summary: When Duck decides to make a jack-o'-lantern, he and his friends Pig and Mouse are in for a scary adventure.
ISBN 978-0-06-169284-0 (trade bdg.) — ISBN 978-0-06-169285-7 (lib. bdg.)
[1. Pumpkin—Fiction. 2. Jack-o-lanterns—Fiction. 3. Ducks—Fiction. 4. Pigs—Fiction. 5. Mice—Fiction.] I. Title.
PZ7.T36694Pu 2011 2010007029
[E]—dc22 CIP
AC

18 SCP 5
❖
First Edition

Pumpkin Trouble

Jan Thomas

HARPER
An Imprint of HarperCollinsPublishers

This will be GREAT!

I can't wait to show Pig and Mouse my jack-o'-lantern!
They'll be **SO** surprised!

Just one last seed...

Whoops!!
Uh-oh!

This isn't good.

Can anyone help me?

Pig? Mouse? Are you there?

Helloooooooooooo?

Argghhhh!
It's a **PUMPKIN**
MONSTER!!

A PUMPKIN MONSTER?!

WHERE?!

Oh no! It's chasing us!

It's chasing us?
HELLLPPP!!!

Quick! Hide behind the barn!

What barn?

SMASH

DUCK?!

LOOK! Duck battled the Pumpkin Monster and **WON**!!
I **DID**?

HURRAY for DUCK!!

I'll make a
jack-o'-lantern
to celebrate!

I wish Duck were here to see this GREAT jack-o'-lantern.
Where IS Duck?

Uh . . . can I get a little help?